J   6/16/10
Sneve, Virginia Driving Hawk
        The Chichi Hoohoo Bogeyman

DATE DUE

DEMCO 128-5046

SNEVE, VIRGINIA DRIVING HA
THE CHICHI HOOHOO BOGEYMAN /

C2008.

The
Chichi Hoohoo
Bogeyman

New Edition

Virginia Driving Hawk Sneve

With a new introduction by the author

drawings by Nadema Agard

UNIVERSITY OF NEBRASKA PRESS
LINCOLN AND LONDON

FOR MY COUSINS

Library of Congress Cataloging-in-Publication Data
Sneve, Virginia Driving Hawk.
The chichi hoohoo bogeyman / Virginia Driving Hawk Sneve;
with a new introduction by the author; drawings by Nadema Agard.
p. cm.
ISBN 978-0-8032-1745-4 (pbk.: alk. paper)
1. Dakota Indians—Juvenile fiction. [1. Dakota Indians—Fiction.
2. Indians of North America—Fiction.] I. Agard, Nadema. II. Title.
PZ7.S679Ch 2008
[Fic]—dc22   2008001815

Contents

Introduction

Ever since Europeans arrived in the Americas, Native tribes have been adapting new cultural elements to their existing traditions. This is the story of how three Native girls blend different concepts into a new imagery.

The bogeyman is an imaginary figure used by white parents to discipline their children. Native Americans have similar spirits that, over the years, have come to have the same characteristics as the bogeyman.

When Sioux bands were in enemy territory, their safety often depended upon keeping silent. The children learned to restrain their cries by being threatened with a *chichi*, an invisible being that represented the enemy. Children were also told that the *chichi* was the cause of unusual events that could not be explained logically. In contemporary times the *chichi* is used to discipline children in the same manner as the bogeyman. But because the Sioux have retained a strong belief in the supernatural, the *chichi* is also treated as a frightening figure associated with other-worldly events.

The Hopi have *kachinas*, spirits that represent important aspects of Hopi life. At different times of the year, masked Hopi men dress as *kachinas* and participate in ceremonies. One visits children to check on their behavior. The costumed man bursts into homes and pounds a staff on the floor while loudly proclaiming, "*Hoohoo!*" and so the children call him *hoohoo*. During the rest of the year, Hopi parents use the *hoohoo* to discipline their children in the same way whites use the bogeyman and Sioux the *chichi*.

Family Tree

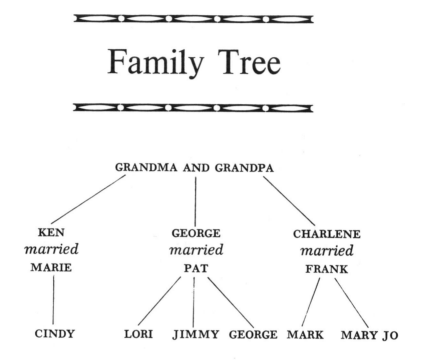

GRANDMA AND GRANDPA

KEN
married
MARIE

GEORGE
married
PAT

CHARLENE
married
FRANK

CINDY

LORI JIMMY GEORGE MARK MARY JO

1

Mesa Warning

Mary Jo linked arms with her two cousins as they walked up the hill toward the River House where their Sioux grandparents lived. The deep shadows and soft light of early evening blended under the willows and elms along the river. The silence was broken only by the sharp chirps of the crickets hiding in the underbrush.

Mary Jo could just see the outlines of the house as it sat nestled under the trees at the end of the graveled drive which led off the paved road north of town.

Suddenly, she heard a piercing scream behind her and a voice which said, "Look out! A chichi!"

Startled, Mary Jo lurched forward while Cindy and Lori raced toward the grown-ups seated around the picnic table in the shadow of the house. The table was lit only by the light filtering through the kitchen window and screen door.

"What's wrong?" Grandpa asked.

Cindy and Lori were giggling but Mary Jo, who had now caught up with her cousins, turned and pointed an accusing finger at Mark, her brother, who was laughing behind them. "He scared us!"

"Just getting the girls in the right mood for a ghost story," Mark chortled. "Just a joke."

"You startled all of us," scolded Frank, his father. "Now sit down and be quiet. I don't think the ghost story we're about to hear is any joke."

Mary Jo seated herself between Lori and Cindy. Despite the gentle golden light given off by the window, she could see that Lori's face was hard and tense.

She studied her Uncle George as he lit a cigarette. The indirect window light left shadows in his eyes and the hollows of his cheeks. He sipped a cup of coffee as he looked around to see if everyone was in place. Then he spoke.

"The reason we are here this summer is because I've taken a new job in Aberdeen. I'll have to go find us a house to live in while Pat and the kids stay here.

"Ever since Pat and I got married, except for the summers we've spent at the River House, we've lived with the Hopis on the mesa. In fact, we used to live in the same house as Pat's parents. As a result we've been very close to Pat's folks—not only her parents, but all of her relatives.

"The Hopis, living in their pueblos on the mesa, isolated from other societies, have kept their traditions alive and are proud of them. They are reluctant to accept strangers in their midst—even Indians of other tribes. I've been lucky as a Sioux to have been treated as one of them. The Hopis are also reluctant to let any of their people leave.

"Oh, many of their people go away to school, but the mesa is still considered home. If one of the tribe moves away, something is lost.

"Before we came up here we spent a week with Pat's

parents on the mesa. When we told them we were moving to Aberdeen, they were unhappy and tried to talk us out of leaving. The last night we were there, Pat's father said that the whole clan was praying that we would change our minds. When so many put their minds to one purpose, he said, the spirits hear and will intervene."

Mary Jo felt a shiver touch her back and she clutched Lori's cold hand.

"I laughed," Uncle George said, "but I knew he was serious so I asked, 'How will we know when the spirits intervene?' He replied very solemnly, 'You will know.' I knew he believed every word he said."

Uncle George paused to light another cigarette. It was so still in the backyard that Mary Jo was afraid to breathe. He shook out his match and continued.

"We went to bed and I went right to sleep. The next thing I knew, Pat was shaking me awake. 'Our car horn is honking,' she said. I jumped out of bed knowing that night noises aren't liked on the mesa. I ran into the dark living room, stumbling over furniture and fumbling to unlock the front door.

"Outside, the horn was blaring loudly and I cussed it for shorting out in the middle of the night. I reached the car and then, just as I started to lift the hood, the horn stopped.

"I cussed some more and went back to bed. I looked at my watch and saw that it was just a few minutes past midnight. I went to sleep and then—it seemed only seconds later —the horn was honking again. This time when I ran outside, I noticed that the porch light was on. But as I got to the car the horn fell silent.

"Now I was mad. I woke the whole apartment. Lori had heard the first noise," he looked at his daughter who nodded, "and the second, but the boys had slept through it. Pat and her folks had heard it too, but didn't have any idea what started it. I was sure someone was playing a joke but couldn't figure out why. It was a little after one o'clock when we all went back to bed.

"I had no trouble getting to sleep when I'll be darned if it didn't happen again. Same way. The front door locked, porch light on, and the horn stopping just as I touched the car.

"I didn't have to wake anybody this time. Everyone, except the boys, was up and nobody knew anything about how it happened. I was furious. I accused Pat's parents of playing tricks to make me think the 'spirits' were causing it." Uncle George sighed and shook his head. "They calmly denied it and we all went back to bed. It was after two this time. Nothing else happened and the next morning we left.

"We drove to Albuquerque, where we were staying overnight with friends. We had supper and went to bed because we wanted to make an early start the next day to drive straight through to Pine Ridge.

"Pat and I hadn't talked about the events of the night before—we didn't want to frighten the children—and we didn't tell our friends. But at midnight, right in that Albuquerque suburb, I'll be darned if the car's horn didn't start blowing again. I heard it first and got up. I had to fumble at the unfamiliar lock on the front door and as I went outside, I saw that the porch and garage lights were both on.

"Our friends heard the car horn too, but couldn't explain what caused it. Well, to shorten the story, it happened twice more. Now I was getting worried.

"At breakfast, I told our friends about how the horn had honked on the mesa. I also told them about how Pat's father had mentioned the possibility of the Hopi spirits' intervention. This was the first time Lori heard about her grandfather's prediction." Uncle George smiled at Lori. "She suggested in her quiet way that maybe the spirits—remember she's half Hopi—were trying to warn us to be careful on our drive to South Dakota."

Mary Jo felt Lori squirm with embarrassment and heard Cindy giggle on the other side. Everyone chuckled and Grandma poured more coffee for Uncle George.

"So," Uncle George began again, "before we left Albuquerque I called brother Ken at Pine Ridge on the Sioux reservation even though it was five o'clock in the morning. I told him that we were leaving for his place and that if we weren't there by midnight, to call the highway patrol to see if we had had an accident."

Laughter went around the table and continued as George, a normally fast driver, told how he had stayed at the speed limit all the way to Pine Ridge. He wouldn't let Pat drive because she was more nervous than he was.

"It was late and I was beat when we got to Pine Ridge," George went on. "Ken and Marie were still up, worried and waiting for us, and Cindy was in bed. Of course, the same thing happened in Pine Ridge that had occurred on the mesa and in Albuquerque. We went to bed just before midnight. I wasn't even asleep yet when the car horn blared. Three times—the same way.

"I raised hell with Ken. I accused him of playing a joke because I had told him what had happened before. But he and Marie swore up and down that they had done nothing. And because they're both Sioux they argued that it was doubtful a Hopi spirit would have followed us into Sioux territory.

"In the morning, I watched Ken go over my car. He knows more about automobiles than I'll ever know. But," and he paused for emphasis, "there was nothing wrong with the car. I had hoped that there was a simple malfunction that would cause the horn to short and honk by itself, although that wouldn't explain why it stopped the minute I touched the car. But there was nothing."

Everyone sat silently when George quit talking. Mary Jo watched Grandpa get up and walk stiffly toward the river and then back again. Her father knocked dead ashes from his pipe and looked thoughtfully at George. Cindy wiggled restlessly, but Lori was sitting very still, staring hollowly into the darkness.

"What can it mean?" asked Frank.

Uncle George shook his head. "I don't know. But if it happens again tonight, Pat says we're going back to the mesa."

Frank stood up. "I'm glad I'm not sleeping here. You'd probably accuse me of honking the horn," he laughed. "All that us white guys have to worry about is the bogeyman."

But Uncle George didn't laugh. "The bogeyman, the Sioux chichi, and the Hopi kachina or hoohoo are similar. I've often wondered if these imaginary figures were invented to explain the puzzling things which happen in our lives. All cultures seem to have them; they just have different names."

"I'm a nonbeliever, George," Frank said. "There has to be a reason for anything unusual."

"Mom," Mary Jo asked. "Can I stay here tonight?"

"No, Mary Jo," her mother answered. "I know you girls wouldn't get to sleep until late and Cindy and Lori must be tired after the long drive from Pine Ridge. We must go home to our own house."

"But," protested Mary Jo, "I want to know if the car horn blows again."

"We all want to know if that happens," Charlene said as she moved toward the driveway. "And if it does, I'm sure Grandma will call us first thing in the morning. Now say good-night. We have to go home."

2

Chichi Hoohoo Bogeyman

It wasn't until after lunch that Mary Jo rode her bike down to the River House. Her mother had let her sleep late, so by the time she had cleaned her room and helped Charlene with the laundry, it was lunchtime.

Grandma had called and said that the horn hadn't honked the night before. As Mary Jo rode her bike out of town, she thought about Uncle George's strange story. Her father had only grunted when she asked him what it meant.

Then he had said, "Strange things happen to people all the time. I'm sure that we'll find out what made the horn honk. In the meantime, there's no need to worry. It probably won't happen again."

But Mary Jo did not feel worried. Just curious. In fact, she hadn't even thought much about Uncle George's story until now. She had been too busy planning things for the cousins to do during the rest of the week.

She waved at Grandpa as she passed him in the green alfalfa field. He was cutting hay, his familiar straw hat pulled low over his eyes; his thin, lithe body vibrating in the seat of the tractor. He had to spend many hours working the small farm of prairie land that yielded such rich alfalfa. But no matter how busy he was with his chores, he always found time to spend with her. She remembered the times they had explored the edge of the river, looking for arrowheads. One time they had found an old red stone pipe. The stem had rotted away, but Grandpa had made a new one and hung it on the living room wall.

He had promised to teach her how to drive the tractor when she was older. Mary Jo wondered if she'd have to wait until she was an old lady! She was sure that Mark had learned when he was eleven. "Boys always get to do things sooner than girls," she thought with disgust. But she decided not to mention it to Grandpa while the cousins were visiting because then Cindy would hog the tractor. "Cindy can be so bossy—and it is irritating that Lori goes along with almost everything Cindy does," she thought to herself.

Mary Jo turned her bike into the driveway of the River House. As she rode past, she ran her hand along the white fence trimmed with colorful geometric Sioux shapes. Then she saw Cindy and Lori sitting at the picnic table busily weaving yarn loops through some kind of a small square loom.

"What are you doing?" she asked as she got closer. She stopped to shake a rattle at baby George, who was sitting on a blanket near the table. He gurgled at her, grabbed the rattle, and tried to put it in his mouth.

"We're babysitting," Cindy said waving at George and two-year-old Jimmy, who was playing in an old tractor tire that served as a sandbox. "Grandma and Aunt Pat are washing diapers in the basement and we gotta watch the boys so they don't wander off and fall in the river."

"But what are you making?" Mary Jo asked as she watched the cousins hook the brightly colored loops over nails that were in the frame of the little square looms.

Lori held hers up for Mary Jo to see. "Grandpa made these for us—there's one for you too. We're making potholders for Grandma."

Cindy handed Mary Jo an empty loom. "Grandma says she needs new potholders, but I know that's just an excuse to give us something to do so we'll stay out of trouble."

"Show me how you do it," said Mary Jo.

"It's easy." Lori stopped her work to instruct Mary Jo.

"I don't think it's so much fun," said Cindy as her slim fingers struggled with the yarn.

"You hurry too much, Cindy, that's why your lines get crooked and lumpy."

The three girls sat busily working, only pausing to lift baby George back on the blanket when he crawled off to look for a stray bug.

"So nothing happened last night?" asked Mary Jo while her fingers moved easily back and forth.

"Lori and I didn't hear anything," Cindy answered.

"We'd have woken up for sure if the car horn had honked as loudly as before," said Lori.

"Why do you suppose it didn't happen here?" asked Mary Jo.

"I know. It's because those old Hopi spirits get weak up here in Sioux land," Cindy suggested as she pushed the loom away from her.

"But it happened in Pine Ridge where there's more Sioux than here," Lori argued.

"Well, then it's because there's both white people and Sioux here. That makes it tough for the Hopis," Cindy reasoned. She swung her legs over the bench and waved a loop of yarn at the baby who reached for it. "And that means the Hopi hoohoo ain't as tough as the Sioux chichi or the white bogeyman."

Mary Jo laughed. "You know that there aren't such things as chichis and bogeymen. That's just what grown-ups say to keep little kids like Jimmy from doing things they aren't supposed to. Remember how Grandpa used to tell us that there was a chichi in the bushes along the river when we were little? Well, we believed him and were scared to go down there—but he told us that on purpose so we'd stay away from the water. Then as we got bigger, he let us go down there by ourselves.

"And the bogeyman is the same thing," Mary Jo went on. "When Mark and I were little and went to visit my father's family, Grandma told us a bogeyman lived in the attic so that we wouldn't climb up the steep stairs. But now she lets us go to the attic all of the time. And I bet the hoohoo is like that too," she said to Lori.

Lori looked up from her loom, her fingers still. "Well, kinda," she said thoughtfully. "A hoohoo is a kachina. At certain ceremonies a man wears the hoohoo costume and mask and comes to see if the kids have been good. I used to think that the hoohoo was *real*. I guess he *is* more real than a chichi or bogeyman because we can see him."

"But you don't believe there's such a thing now do you?" Mary Jo asked.

Lori picked up her loom and didn't answer right away.

"I don't know," she said hesitantly.

The other two girls were quiet. They were all thinking about the mysterious way the car horn had started by itself. Then Cindy started to laugh.

"I only have one to worry about," she giggled, "but you guys have two."

Mary Jo and Lori looked at Cindy. "What are you talking about?" Cindy was doubled up with laughter.

"Tell us what's so funny," Mary Jo begged. Cindy was now so carried away that she couldn't even keep her feet on the ground, and Mary Jo thought for sure she would fall off the chair.

Finally she said breathlessly, "I'm all Sioux so I just have a chichi to be scared of. But you," she giggled pointing to Mary Jo, "are half-white and half-Sioux so you have a chichi bogeyman. And Lori," she said through twitching lips, "has a chichi hoohoo." Then she was so overcome with her own wit that she fell off the bench and lay laughing beside the baby who promptly crawled onto her stomach.

Cindy's mirth was contagious and before Mary Jo knew it, she was laughing too. She looked over at Lori who gasped between giggles, "They're all kinda the same anyway."

"Yeah," agreed Mary Jo. She hooted loudly as a thought struck her. "When we grow up we can scare our kids with the chichi hoohoo bogeyman."

The girls were convulsed with laughter. The baby gurgled happily, waving his arms up and down like a young bird learning to fly. Jimmy came over carrying his sand pail, stumbled and dumped sand in Cindy's face and hair. This brought louder peals from Lori and Mary Jo as Cindy

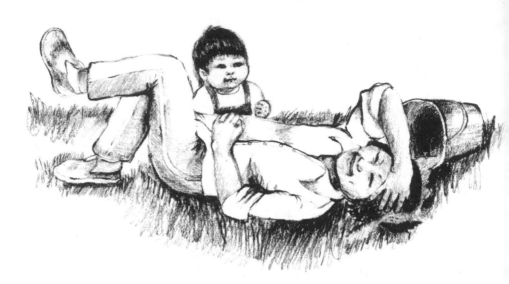

pushed the baby aside and jumped up to brush off the sand. "Jimmy," she scolded still giggling, "the chichi hoohoo bogeyman is gonna get you for that!" Then she lunged at Jimmy who turned and ran screaming toward the house.

"Oh," Lori wailed, "the baby's eating sand," and she dashed to pick him up.

"What's going on?" asked Grandma as she and Aunt Pat came out of the house, hauling Jimmy and loaded down with a bucket of wet diapers.

"Jimmy dumped sand all over me," Cindy said, not laughing now as she wiped sand from her face and shook it from her hair.

"He didn't do it on purpose," said Mary Jo. By this time, Jimmy was beginning to calm down and made another grab for the sand pail.

Pat stooped to brush sand from Jimmy's clothes. "Why is it when you three are together some dumb thing like this always happens?"

"The baby has sand all over him too," Grandma said, taking George from Lori. "Get the blanket, Lori, and shake the sand back in the tire. Cindy, go fetch your hairbrush and get the sand out of your hair. You'll probably have to shampoo it. I know we're going to have to bathe the baby," she said crossly. "You should be old enough to take care of the little ones without causing so much trouble." She carried the baby into the house. Pat followed with Jimmy.

Mary Jo didn't even look at Lori as they cleaned up the sand from around the picnic table. She still felt like laughing but stiffled her giggles because she knew Grandma and Aunt Pat were angry.

The two girls sat working at their looms until Cindy came out of the house, her short hair wet from a quick shampoo. "Let's get out of here," she said. "I don't want to mess with those old looms any more. Let's go for a walk."

The girls put the looms and yarn back in the box and started walking toward the river. "Where are you going?" called Grandma.

"Can we walk up to the old fur post?" Cindy asked.

"If you stay on this side of the river and don't wade across to the fort. Even if the water looks shallow there, you might step in a deep hole."

"We won't," said Lori as they took off toward the river.

They slowed to a walk as they reached the path by the riverbank which led upstream. Cindy walked ahead of the others who followed in single file beneath the overhanging branches of the willows and elm trees. Mary Jo felt as if she were walking through a green tunnel. The only sound she heard was the soft rustle of their feet in the brush and an occasional gurgle from the river as it flowed around a fallen tree.

"I wish we were boys," Cindy broke the silence, her voice muted by the dense foliage.

"Why?" asked Mary Jo, as she picked up a twig and tossed it into the water.

"Because then we could go wherever we wanted along the river and nobody would tell us not to do this or stay away from that. We could even go swimming and everybody would say 'that's okay.' Boys are supposed to do things like that. But if we did—" Cindy snorted with disgust.

"That's right. Mark swims in the river all of the time with the boys from town, but I'm not supposed to. Grandma would let us wade across the river if we were boys, 'cause she'd know boys would do it anyway."

"So, let's," said Cindy.

"What?" Mary Jo bumped smack into Cindy.

"Wade across the river."

"But Grandma told us not to," said Lori.

"Haven't you been listening to what we've been saying? If we were boys nobody would tell us not to."

"That's right." Mary Jo had to admit that Cindy had a point. "Mark and his friends used to wade over to the fort and play there all of the time."

The girls had reached a spot on the river where the trees grew farther back on either side, leaving a wide grassy area which ended in a narrow sandy beach. The Big Sioux was not a wide river and followed a gentle, twisting course to where it joined the Missouri River farther to the south. There were many areas like this along its shoreline.

The girls looked across the river to the grassy ruins of an old fort. Grandpa had told them that Frenchmen had built the fort in the early 1760's and that nomadic Sioux had camped there. White men had also used it for trading posts.

Cindy sat down and began to remove her shoes and socks. "Well, you two can stay here but I'm going to wade across."

Mary Jo hesitated only a moment and then sat and untied her sneakers. But Lori wrung her hands. "Grandma told us not to," she wailed. "And Mom will be mad if she finds out we didn't mind." She didn't want to be left behind though, and was soon barefoot.

Mary Jo rolled her jeans above her knees, but Cindy stood to take hers off.

"Cindy—," Mary Jo was shocked at the thought of them crossing the river half-naked.

"What's the matter?" Cindy asked. "There's nobody around except us—and besides, I got panties on. If we get our jeans wet, Grandma will know we've been in the river."

Mary Jo and Lori looked at each other and giggled as they removed their jeans.

Mary Jo followed Cindy into the muddy river. She could feel the cold water swirl around her ankles, and moved slowly forward into the deepening water. At first the stream was as high as her knees. But when she approached the middle, the water slapped against her hips, nearly knocking her down. Mary Jo looked back and saw Lori struggling to keep her footing. She reached back to grab her hand.

The current was tugging at them violently. Mary Jo braced her body against the strong pull of the river. She felt like a boat being yanked from its mooring by the wind. Then the water was around her knees again and she breathed more easily. They walked out onto the sand.

"Ooh," Lori shivered. "That's deep and I was scared for a minute I might drown."

"It wasn't as deep as I thought," Cindy boasted.

When Mary Jo saw the ruins, she was disappointed. "It doesn't look like a fort—just green bumps."

"Yeah, I know," Cindy agreed. "Last year when Grandpa brought us in the canoe it seemed like there was more."

"That's 'cause Grandpa told us what used to be here," Lori said as she tried to squeeze water from her clinging wet underpants. "We imagined more."

"You're probably right," said Mary Jo.

"Come on," called Cindy. "We might as well look around while we're here."

Mary Jo walked between the sunken indentations in the ground and the large stones that were strewn about randomly —this was all that remained of the old fur post. Cindy moved on toward the trees farther back from the river.

"Watch out!" Mary Jo warned. "There's poison ivy in there."

The girls stopped and looked over the ground under the trees. "There's nothing more to see here," said Lori. "We'd better go back."

"Wait, there's a path." Cindy pointed to a break between the trees where the grass was worn down.

"We really should be getting back," Lori said.

"Oh, come on. This path might lead somewhere interesting," coaxed Cindy.

Mary Jo could see that it wound between the tall tree trunks which stood to either side like brooding giants. She wondered where it led as she followed Cindy into the woods, Lori trailing slowly behind.

The girls moved quietly up the path which turned at the crest of a small hill. Suddenly they found themselves on the edge of the Dakota prairie which rolled away from the tree line of the river. Mary Jo could see what looked like a small gray dwelling in the distance. She walked a little closer to where Cindy had stopped and saw that the path led to a weather-beaten shack.

"I never knew there was a house here," Cindy whispered. "Did you, Mary Jo? Does anyone live here?"

Even as Cindy spoke, Mary Jo saw a man come out of the shack. She drew back into the shelter of the trees as he paused and looked down the path. He wore shapeless trousers and a tattered, long-sleeved blue shirt. Gray strands of hair straggled about his face. He raised a hand to brush it back and Mary Jo saw his mouth moving as if he were talking to himself. He moved in a halting, jerky, sideways fashion and he was coming toward the trees.

"Run!" Cindy commanded in a loud whisper.

The girls fled back to the river through the trees. Mary Jo raced to keep up with Cindy, leaving Lori to follow behind as best she could.

Mary Jo stopped in horror as she heard Lori scream and call out, "Help! My hair!"

Mary Jo turned and saw Lori struggling to free one of her braids which had caught on a low hanging branch. Quickly Mary Jo freed her, grabbed her hands and pulled

her toward the river. All three girls splashed noisily across. Several times Mary Jo had to hoist Lori to her feet since the current was too much for her short legs.

Mary Jo was gasping for breath when they reached the other side. She scooped up her jeans, shoes and socks and ran down the path toward home.

"Wait," Lori panted. "I got to stop."

Mary Jo slowed down and tried to catch her breath. She looked anxiously at Cindy to see what they should do next, but Cindy looked as frightened as Mary Jo felt.

"You stay with Lori," Mary Jo told Cindy. "I'll go see if he followed us."

She walked cautiously back to the edge of the trees and peered across the river. The man was there. He gazed across the water but didn't seem to see her. Mary Jo noticed that he carried a fishing pole and a can of worms. He looked around and then seemed satisfied that he was alone. He smiled as he moved toward the water. Mary Jo withdrew farther into the trees, her heart thumping wildly. Many of the man's teeth were missing and his smile made his straggly hair and wrinkled face more menacing than ever. But he only moved in his crab-like walk to the shore where he stopped, took a worm from the can, baited his hook and threw his line in the water.

Mary Jo relaxed and ran quietly back along the path to where her cousins waited. "It's okay," she assured them. "He's only fishing."

Cindy and Lori were standing in the path not daring to sit down and get their wet underpants muddy.

"Who is he?" Cindy asked.

"I don't know, but he sure is weird," Mary Jo answered.

"We can ask Grandpa when we get home," said Lori.

"Are you kidding? We can't ask anyone. If we did, they'd know we waded across the river," Cindy sneered.

"What are we going to do?" moaned Lori. "They'll know anyway 'cause we're all wet."

"Just our panties," Cindy was calm, "and we'll take them off. Then when we put our dry jeans on no one will know."

"What'll we do with our wet panties?"

"I'll take them home and throw them in our dryer," Mary Jo volunteered. "Mom will never know 'cause I'm always washing and drying my own clothes."

"You are?" Lori asked.

"Sure, I had to learn how since Mom teaches school." Mary Jo stripped off her wet underpants and pulled on her jeans.

"That's great," Cindy said, wringing the water from her panties. She led the way back toward the River House.

"Don't leave me behind!" Lori's face looked tense and reminded Mary Jo of the evening around the picnic table when they heard Uncle George's story. "I was so frightened," Lori went on. "That man was so awful looking, and when my braid got stuck I knew he had caught me."

"I bet you thought the chichi hoohoo bogeyman got you," Cindy giggled.

But Lori didn't laugh. "That's what I *was* thinking about."

Cindy snickered, "Boy, are you silly."

But Mary Jo only gave a weak grin. "I don't think it's so funny. I thought the same thing when I saw him. Maybe it was 'cause we had been talking about chichis and the stuff that happened to Uncle George."

Cindy only laughed harder. "Okay, that's what we'll call the man—our real own chichi hoohoo bogeyman!"

As the River House came into view Lori asked, "Mary Jo, how are you going to carry our wet underpants home without Mom and Grandpa seeing them?"

Mary Jo thought aloud. "I've got my windbreaker in my bike basket. If I can get it I can wrap them up in there. I know—you stay here, hide the panties, and I'll go up and get my bike. We can have fun riding it fast down the hill— remember how we did last year? Then I'll get a chance to hide 'em when I have to go home."

Mary Jo got her bike from the house and while Lori watched, she and Cindy took turns riding the bike swiftly down the slope and skidding it into a turn just before they reached the river. They did it several times until Aunt Pat called them to stop before they fell in the river and got wet.

"That's what we should have done," gasped Cindy. "We could have fallen in the river right in front of the house and that would explain our wet underpants—we'd be wet all over."

"It's too late now," Mary Jo said, "and I got to go home." She wrapped the wet undergarments in her windbreaker while her cousins stood between her and the view from the house.

3

Canoe

Mary Jo had no difficulty sneaking the wet undergarments into the house. She bundled up the panties with the rest of her dirty clothes and put them all in the automatic washer. She had to tell her mother that she'd gotten the clothes muddy playing at the River House.

"I'm glad you're washing the clothes right away before the mud sets," Charlene said.

Mary Jo couldn't look her mother in the eyes. She mumbled something about getting a snack and bolted for the kitchen.

The next day Cindy and Lori came for the night. The three girls went to an old Western which they had already seen. The movie house had been around for years and the narrow rows of worn seats were quickly filled. The girls sat quietly, munching on popcorn, when suddenly Cindy let out a whoop. She cheered as the movie Indians attacked a wagon train. Then she booed when the cavalry drove them off. Mary Jo couldn't help but giggle until she heard "shh's" and "be quiets" from the other people in the audience. Then the owner of the small theater came down the aisle toward the girls. Mary Jo scrunched way down in her seat, but he stopped and shone his flashlight on them. "You must be quiet," he said sternly, "or else you'll have to leave."

"Okay, okay," Cindy said, "keep your pants on."

Cindy turned and grabbed Mary Jo. "Let's get out of here," she whispered.

Mary Jo hung her head as the three girls left the theater, disrupting the people in the other seats as they plowed toward the aisle. When they reached the sidewalk, Mary Jo turned and faced Cindy squarely. "How could you talk to that man the way you did? I could have died."

"Oh, pooh!" Cindy scoffed. "You two are sissies. I suppose you'll tell Aunt Charlene and Uncle Frank."

"No, I won't," retorted Mary Jo. " 'Cause they wouldn't let me go to the movies for a month. I don't know if I want to anyway—all my friends were there. They must think I'm the biggest dummy in the whole world."

When the girls got home they told Charlene they left the movie early because it was boring.

Mary Jo led the girls to her room. All she could think about was how much she wanted Cindy to go back to the River House. She looked at the camp cot set up next to the double bed. "You can sleep in the cot, Cindy," scolded Mary Jo.

"I don't care. In fact I'll sleep on the floor. Beds are for chickens," said Cindy tossing back her hair.

Mary Jo opened some potato chips and offered them to Lori. Then she whispered something in Lori's ear and they both looked at Cindy and started giggling.

Cindy sat down on the cot. She looked around the room

and then at her cousins. "Okay," she muttered. "I'm sorry about the way I acted in the movie theater . . . But you thought it was funny when I was cheering the Indians and booing the whites in that dumb show."

Mary Jo had to smile. She never could stay angry with Cindy for very long.

"That was a stupid movie," she agreed. "Everybody in it was stupid—especially the Indians."

"Indians are always stupid and dumb in movies. That's why everyone thinks Indians should act that way in real life." Cindy got up from the cot, stuck one finger behind her head, hopped around in a fake war dance and rapidly patted her mouth with her other hand.

"Whoo, whoo, whoo," she chanted. Then she stopped, folded her arms across her chest and pulled her face into a stern, stoic mask. "Me heap Chief Big Mouth. Giveum me tato chips and firewater or me scalpum you!" She lunged toward the double bed with a bloodcurdling whoop as she grabbed Lori's braids. Then she grabbed a bottle of pop, took a long swig and staggered back to the cot. "Ugh!" she belched. "Firewater good."

"You're better than any movie," giggled Lori.

"And you're right," Mary Jo said. "That's how people think Indians are supposed to talk."

"I know," said Lori. "Tourists who come to the mesa are surprised that we can speak English."

"Ugh," Cindy reached for the potato chip bag. "When I grow up I'm going to be real smart and use only big words when I talk. Nobody will dare call me a dumb Injun. Is this all the chips?" she asked shaking the empty bag.

"Mom only gave me the one bag, I don't think she wanted us to eat any more, especially since we had popcorn at the movie. She's afraid we'll get stomachaches and be sick in the middle of the night."

"Don't you get tired of being treated like a little kid all the time?" Cindy asked, wadding up the potato chip bag and throwing it in the direction of the wastebasket. "Someone's always telling us what we can or can't do. We're not babies any more. We're eleven—at least I am."

"Lori and I are almost eleven too," said Mary Jo.

"I wonder what we'll get for our special present this year?" Lori mused knowing that whenever the three cousins celebrated their birthday together, they were given a surprise treat. "Do you suppose they'll take us back to the amusement park in Sioux Falls? I liked that."

"I know what would be fun. Let's ask Grandpa if we can take the canoe on the river by ourselves," Cindy suggested. "You know he promised to let us when we got bigger. I think we're big enough now."

"That's a great idea," said Lori, "although it might be kind of scary."

"You're scared of everything," Cindy teased.

"I'm not either."

"Let's ask Grandpa tomorrow," interrupted Mary Jo. "He ought to let us because he let Mark take the canoe when he was our age."

"Okay, girls," Charlene called outside the bedroom door. "You better get to sleep now."

The cousins put their pajamas on. Cindy crawled into the sleeping bag on the cot but Mary Jo protested. "You and

Lori can sleep in the bed. You're my guests and I'll sleep on the cot."

"No," Cindy said snuggling into the bag. "I'll sleep here by myself. I have to share a bed with Lori at Grandma's and she's always taking all of the covers."

"Well, you kick and wiggle all night long," Lori complained as she sat on the bed and began to unbraid her long hair.

"Can't you do your hair in the dark?" Cindy grumbled. "You take so long unbraiding it, brushing it and then braiding it again. Turn off the light."

"Oh, cover up your head, Cindy," Mary Jo said. "I want to watch Lori. I wish I had long black hair instead of my icky, brown curly stuff." She watched Lori brush her waist-long hair and then plait it into one fat braid.

"You wouldn't like it," Cindy said. "It's too much work having to do it every night so it won't be all tangled in the morning. And then it has to be done all over again in the morning. It hurts and its heavy. That's why I cut mine off."

Mary Jo lifted Lori's braid. "Gosh, it is heavy. Does it give you a headache?"

"Sometimes," Lori said. "But I don't mind. I could never cut it off because Mom and Dad say a Sioux-Hopi girl is supposed to have long hair."

"Pooh!" scoffed Cindy. "You're just scared the chichi hoohoo bogeyman will get you if you cut your hair."

"I am not!" Lori retorted. "Besides, you look funny with your hair so short."

"Oh, let's go to sleep," said Mary Jo not wanting another fight and turned off the light by the bed.

*

Charlene drove the girls to the River House after lunch the next day. Mary Jo told her that she wanted Grandpa to let them take the canoe out by themselves. "Is that all right, Mom?" she asked.

"That's up to your grandfather," Charlene answered. "But if he lets you, be careful."

Charlene went with the girls into the house and reported to Grandma and Aunt Pat that the cousins had behaved themselves well in town. "Is there anything I can get for the picnic tonight?" she asked Grandma.

"Just bring a salad," said Grandma. "We'll eat about six. George should be back from Aberdeen by then."

"Where's Grandpa?" Cindy asked.

"He took Jimmy to the bedroom to see if he could get him to take a nap," Grandma said. "I bet he fell asleep himself."

"No, he didn't," Grandpa laughed as he came into the kitchen. "But Jimmy did and baby George is still sleeping, so you girls be quiet."

"Grandpa," Mary Jo asked, "will you let us take the canoe out by ourselves as our birthday treat?"

"Please?" Cindy added. "You let Mark do it when he was eleven."

"Oh, I don't think that's such a good idea," Grandma broke in. "Besides, I think Mark was bigger and stronger when he was your age."

"No, he wasn't," Mary Jo argued. "We're just as big as he was, aren't we Mom?"

Charlene nodded. "You and Cindy are, I'm sure. Lori might have a little trouble because she's smaller, but then she's the most sensible." Charlene winked at Lori. "Do you think the girls can handle the canoe, Dad?" she asked Grandpa. "I know I was worried about Mark when he first took it out alone, but he got along all right."

"Well," Grandpa said going to the door, "let's see how you do."

"Be careful," Charlene called as she walked toward her car. "I'll be back for the picnic and I don't want to find you all wet from falling in the river."

Grandpa got three life jackets from the garage and insisted that the girls put them on. Then they helped him carry the fiber glass canoe to the river. He put on a larger jacket from the canoe and then they launched it.

"Be careful," he cautioned. "Lift the canoe so that it is not dragging on the ground and push it out into the water."

He then showed them how to get into the canoe. "Crouch and hold onto each side as you get in," he said as he moved slowly to the bow end in the water. "A canoe will tip easily because of its rounded bottom, so don't ever stand in it or get too much weight on one side." He sat facing the girls on the shore where Cindy and Mary Jo were steadying the canoe. "Okay," he said, "Mary Jo, you first."

Mary Jo had been canoeing with Grandpa many times before. Even though she knew how to paddle, he had her practice steering in the stern and then reversing, so that her end became the bow. He had Cindy do the same thing but took Lori out alone with him. She needed more practice since her shorter arms made paddling difficult for her.

At last Grandpa was satisfied that the girls could handle the canoe alone. "Okay," he said, steadying the canoe so that all three girls could get in. "You can go for a ride alone, but keep the life jackets on. This river is shallow enough so that you can wade in some places, but in other spots it's way over your heads. You must promise to keep the jackets on."

"We promise," said Mary Jo.

Then she climbed back into the boat but before she knelt in position, Grandpa gave the canoe a sharp push and then jerked it around. The craft yawed wildly out into the water. Mary Jo grabbed for one side and suddenly she was in the river, the canoe was upside down, and the paddles were floating downstream.

Mary Jo had landed flat on her face in the shallows and stood up with mud covering her front. She looked with hurt

surprise at Grandpa, who was smiling, and realized that he had deliberately upset them. She turned and waded out to the drifting canoe which Lori was clinging to for dear life. Cindy had swum downstream to retrieve the paddles.

"Okay," Grandpa called, "right the canoe."

It was difficult to do. Mary Jo took one of the paddles from Cindy, but neither was strong enough to turn the canoe with one arm. And Lori was no help since she kept holding onto the canoe. Cindy finally made Lori hold the paddles. "You won't go under," she instructed. "Tread water and don't let the paddles get away."

Finally Mary Jo and Cindy managed to push the canoe into shallow water and turned it over. It's bottom was filled with water. Lori finally kicked herself to where she could stand up and she angrily shook one of the paddles at her grandfather. "You did that on purpose. That was mean!"

"That's right," Grandpa smiled. "I had to see if you girls really could handle the canoe if you got in trouble. You did just fine," he said proudly. "Now you can take it out by yourselves."

"But we're all wet," complained Lori as the girls waded ashore. "And the life jackets are soggy and heavy."

Mary Jo and Cindy were laughing as they pulled the canoe ashore and tipped the water out. "Oh, Grandpa," Mary Jo said, "you really scared us."

"I meant to." Grandpa's eyes twinkled. "Now go get dry clothes on. I have three more life jackets in the garage— that is, if you still want to go out alone."

Mary Jo and Cindy wanted to but Lori said, "No, I think I'll stay here and help Grandma get ready for the picnic."

"Oh, come on, Lori," Mary Jo urged as the girls changed into dry clothes.

"But I wouldn't be any help. You both got mad at me when Grandpa tipped us over."

"We won't tip over again," Mary Jo said as she pulled on her jeans. "Even if we do, we know what to do if it happens."

"And you found out that you can stay afloat and not drown," Cindy coaxed. "So come on."

"Well, okay," Lori finally agreed. "But don't you guys get mad at me if I'm no help in paddling."

The girls hung their wet clothes and life jackets on the clothesline and went back to the canoe.

Grandpa steadied the canoe as they got into it. "Now," he said as he pushed them out into the river, "don't go too far downstream. It's easier to paddle going down but it'll be harder work coming back up."

"Let's go upstream first," Mary Jo said. "Then it won't be so tiring when we come back."

"One more thing," Grandpa called out as the girls paddled away. "Don't try to beach the canoe any place. You might poke a hole in the bottom."

Mary Jo easily matched her paddle strokes with Cindy's. She was surprised at the effortless way the canoe glided through the water. The rhythmic splash of the paddles was lulling and she felt like she was traveling the river for the first time. She glanced back and saw that Lori was smiling as she knelt in the middle and trailed her fingers in the water. Then Mary Jo realized that she was sweating under the warm life jacket. Her arms and shoulders were getting tired and it was getting harder to paddle.

"Can't we slow down a little bit?" she called back to Cindy who was sitting in the stern.

"We can paddle slower," Cindy said, sounding as if she were out of breath, "but we can't stop or we'll drift back downstream."

She was right. As the girls tried to slow their strokes they broke their coordinated rhythm and the current swung the bow to the left. They had lost control.

"What are you doing?" Lori cried and clutched the sides of the rocking canoe. "Watch out! We'll tip over again!"

"Oh, shut up!" Cindy ordered, fighting to keep the bow pointed upstream. "Mary Jo, move your paddle to the right side and hold it there!"

Mary Jo did as Cindy directed and soon they were heading the right way. "Now!" Cindy cried. "Paddle!"

Again they paddled together but it was hard work. "We'll have to turn back," Mary Jo called over her shoulder. "I — I can't keep this up. My arms are getting tired."

"We're almost to the fort," Cindy panted. "Keep going. When we get there we'll rest a while and then go back."

"But Grandpa told us not to beach the canoe," Lori objected. "And what if that scary man comes down?"

"You don't know how hard it is to paddle," Mary Jo gasped as the river widened at the fort site. "I have to rest."

She watched for rocks or branches in the water that might puncture the canoe as they beached it. She climbed out onto dry ground and held the canoe steady as Lori and Cindy joined her. Then they pulled the canoe farther on shore and tied its line to a shrub so it wouldn't float away.

'Whew!" Mary Jo panted as she sank down on the grass and rubbed her aching arms. "That was a lot of work."

"Of course it's work," Cindy said flopping down on her stomach. "But it'll be easier after we get used to it."

Mary Jo and Cindy rested on the ground but Lori wandered around near the canoe. Every once in a while she glanced at the path through the trees.

"What's the matter, Lori," Cindy teased. "Afraid that ol' chichi hoohoo bogeyman will come get you?"

"I don't think that's funny," Lori whined. "What if he's a crazy man or an escaped convict or something? Maybe he's a bad man that does bad things to girls."

"Oh, pooh!" Cindy said. "I bet he's harmless. And even if he were a bad man we could run faster than he can. Remember the funny way he walked?" She jumped to her feet and mimicked the crab-like movements of the strange man.

"Can you see him running?" said Mary Jo and she started running crab-like across the sand.

"Oh, I'm thirsty," Cindy said stopping her imitation. "Let's go see if the chichi hoohoo bogeyman is gone. I saw a pump outside his house the last time we were here."

"You mean go up to his house?" Lori cried in alarm.

"I don't think we should, Cindy," Mary Jo protested. "He might be bad like Lori said. You know we're not supposed to talk to strange men."

"Well, if he's at home we won't talk to him. We'll just come back to the canoe and leave. Come on," Cindy urged, "let's go look." She started toward the path.

Mary Jo felt Lori's hand in hers. "Don't leave me here

alone," Lori whimpered.

"I won't," said Mary Jo, "but we can't let Cindy go up there by herself. Come."

Cindy waited for them by the edge of the trees. Then they started along the path. "See," Cindy whispered as they reached the crest of the hill. She pointed to a rusty iron pump near the house. "Let's go get a drink. He isn't there."

"But he might be in the house," Mary Jo whispered, her throat dry with excitement.

"I'll peek in the window first." Cindy moved toward the shack.

"Cindy, come back," Mary Jo called but when Cindy ignored her, she had no choice but to follow.

Cindy was almost to the pump when suddenly the man came out of the house. As soon as he saw the girls, his hands flew up in front of him. His mouth opened and unintelligible sounds came out. Then he moved toward them, his hair looking more scraggly than ever. Mary Jo noticed with horror that his eyes were bloodshot and that he was carrying a hatchet.

Cindy turned and ran past her cousins. Mary Jo pulled Lori after her and the man followed in a shufflling run. He reached out toward Lori's flying braids. She felt his touch and screamed.

Cindy stopped and looked back as Mary Jo and Lori rushed forward. A fallen branch lay near the path and Cindy picked it up and threw it with all her might at the pursuing man. He stumbled and fell as the branch hit him in the legs.

Quickly the girls ran to the river. Mary Jo pulled Lori

into the rocking canoe while Cindy pushed it out into the deeper water. The current caught it and Cindy was knee-deep before she crawled into the craft. It yawed and shifted under her weight and water splashed over the sides. Mary Jo frantically paddled until she realized they were in danger of running aground on the opposite shore. Cindy almost dropped her paddle in the river before she was able to turn the boat downstream.

They moved swiftly now, paddling only to keep the canoe in the center of the stream and away from the over-hanging branches on shore. Lori was sobbing and Mary Jo felt as if her heart were pounding in her ears. "We have to tell Grandpa about that man," she said.

"Yes," Lori hiccuped between sobs.

"No, we're not!" Cindy said firmly. "If we tell, Grandpa will never let us take the canoe out again."

"But he chased us," Mary Jo protested, "and he almost got Lori."

Lori wept harder.

"Oh, shut up, Lori!" Cindy ordered. "You aren't hurt and we got you away okay. Now listen," she said as the canoe glided downstream. "We're not going to tell. If we do, we won't be able to have anymore fun the rest of the time we stay. Your mom will keep you home, Mary Jo, and Grandma and Aunt Pat will make Lori and me stay close to the house."

"But how are you going to explain your wet shoes and jeans?" Mary Jo asked.

"Well," said Cindy, "we could say that when we turned around at the fort to come home, the canoe got stuck in the sand 'cause it's so shallow there, and I had to get in the water to push us loose. That's sort of true," she added. "I *did* get wet pushing us off the sand on the shore."

"We're never going back to that place again!" Lori stated fiercely as she looked over her shoulder at Cindy.

"We sure aren't!" Mary Jo agreed.

"That's okay with me. I don't care if we never go there again but remember, we're not telling," said Cindy.

Lori quit crying, but huddled miserably in the center of the canoe. Mary Jo dipped her paddle deeply into the water and the canoe leapt forward. She knew they should tell the grown-ups about their encounter with the strange man. What if he were a bad man like Lori said? But Mary Jo also knew that Cindy was right. She felt all twisted up inside and wanted to cry.

It was almost time for the picnic when the girls reached the River House and beached the canoe. They walked slowly up to the house. Mary Jo hated to think of the lies they were going to tell. But the grown-ups did not notice Cindy's wet jeans or Lori's tearstained face. They were crowded around the picnic table listening to Uncle George tell how his car horn had mysteriously honked again the previous night in Aberdeen.

4

Nightmare

Mary Jo awoke and lay rigid in her bed. Her thoughts were a wild confusion of the strange man running after her as she floundered and thrashed in deep water, with the sound of a car horn growling in the background. The door to her room opened and she cowered under the covers as her mother came in.

"Did the thunder wake you up?" Charlene asked quietly as she moved to the open window.

Now Mary Jo heard the distant rumble of an approaching summer storm and saw lightning flickering across the sky through the partly open windows. "It's sprinkling a bit," Charlene said. "I thought I'd better shut the windows in case we get a hard rain." She pulled the shade down and turned to leave the room, then paused by Mary Jo's bed. "Are you all right?"

Mary Jo suddenly wanted to feel her mother's arms around her and be soothed and comforted like when she was a little girl. But she swallowed the lump in her throat and whispered, "I'm okay."

Charlene lingered a moment more. Then she tucked

the covers snugly around Mary Jo and kissed her on the forehead. "Don't let Uncle George's story upset you," she said quietly. "Go back to sleep."

Uncle George's old car horn wasn't the only thing that was distressing Mary Jo. She couldn't stop thinking about the strange man and all of the sneaky disobedient things that she had done that day. And she felt really bothered that she hadn't told Grandpa or her mother about the man.

She moved about restlessly on the mattress, trying to find a more comfortable position for her aching arms and shoulders. "I hope Cindy hurts as much as I do," she thought spitefully. "It's all her fault. The canoe paddling was so strenuous! And Cindy didn't give a hoot about Lori's feelings. Lori was so scared!"

The picnic hadn't been fun either. The grown-ups had been quiet after Uncle George's story about how his car horn had honked again in the same mysterious manner outside his motel room in Aberdeen. They had tried to act as if things were normal but Mary Jo could sense their uneasiness. They hadn't even noticed Cindy slipping into the house to change into dry clothes or Lori's weepy red eyes or her own guilty silence.

And Lori had hardly eaten a thing. The adults hadn't noticed that either. And even Cindy had been quiet. But Cindy didn't care about anything except getting her own way. "Tomorrow," Mary Jo thought to herself, "I'm going to tell. I don't care what Cindy says."

She fell into a fitful sleep which seemed only a few minutes long. Then she awoke again to find her mother standing by the bed. Mary Jo sat up. "What's wrong?" she asked.

"Grandma just called," Charlene said. "During the night Lori had a bad nightmare. After they finally got her awake she was hysterical."

"Oh," breathed Mary Jo, fully awake now. "She was so scared."

"That's not all," Charlene went on, her face set in stern and worried lines. "Cindy's gone."

"Gone?"

"Yes. Sometime early this morning, after everyone had settled back to sleep, she must have left the house. She had been upset by Lori's nightmare and hysterics and said that it was all her fault."

While Mary Jo slipped on her jeans, she thought about how wretched Cindy had been to make her and Lori do all those things and then promise not to tell. Mary Jo shook her head and then tears came.

"It's my fault too, Mom," she wept. "I should have stood up to Cindy 'cause I knew Lori was so scared—I was too. But I didn't have to do what Cindy wanted."

Mary Jo sat down on the bed. Suddenly her mother's arms were wrapped warmly around her.

"I knew something was bothering you last night—even at the picnic you were unusually quiet. But I was so upset by George's experience . . ." She hugged Mary Jo and then stood. "Get dressed. We have to go to the River House."

"Where's Cindy?" Mary Jo asked, wiping away the tears.

"I don't know. Aunt Pat woke up with the baby at about five this morning, and that's when she found Cindy gone. Your dad and Mark are at the house now—I think they're going to look along the river for Cindy."

"Oh," gasped Mary Jo. "What if the chichi hoohoo bogeyman got Cindy."

"The what?"

Mary Jo started to explain but Charlene stopped her. "Wait until we get to the River House. You can tell everybody then."

At the River House they found everyone except Lori and the boys sitting quietly around the kitchen table. Frank took her hand and drew her to him as she entered the kitchen.

"Honey," he said gently, "do you have any idea where Cindy might have gone?"

"No," Mary Jo answered, her voice quavering. "Haven't you found her yet?"

"No," Frank said shaking his head. Then he held her closer to him. "We called the sheriff. He's getting a crew to drag the river."

"Why?" Mary Jo asked, her voice was muffled by her father's shoulder.

"We can't find Cindy any place," Mary Jo looked up as Grandpa spoke and saw that his wrinkled face was tired and looked older. "I'm afraid that she may have fallen in the river in the dark and —," his voice broke and he covered his face with his hands.

"Honey," Frank said calmly to Mary Jo, "it rained last night. The river's up. The bank is soft and slippery—we have to consider the possibility of Cindy . . . ," he broke off and held tightly to Mary Jo who began to weep again with deep wrenching sobs. "Shh," he whispered. "Don't cry so. We don't know—maybe Cindy's just hiding someplace."

"But why did she run away?" Mary Jo pulled away from her father and gazed wildly around the room. Grandma was standing behind Grandpa, her hands on his drooping shoulders. Uncle George sat smoking a cigarette and staring at nothing through the smoke he made. Mark was nervously rolling and unrolling an empty matchbook. Charlene reached over to take Mary Jo's hand. Aunt Pat rose and walked to the kitchen counter to get a tissue to blow her nose.

"Where's Lori?" Mary Jo asked.

Aunt Pat turned. "She's sleeping. She was so hysterical that we gave her one of Grandma's tranquilizers. Her screams woke me up," Aunt Pat went on. "I woke George and we went to the basement where the girls slept. Cindy was holding Lori and trying to wake her up. But she kept screaming and hitting at Cindy and yelling over and over, 'My hair, my hair! Let me go! Let me go!'"

Pat walked back to the table and sat down. "We finally woke her up, but she was so frightened from her nightmare that she started crying and talking wildly about falling in the river, chichis, hoohoos and the bogeyman. She didn't make any sense. She didn't want Cindy near her—she kept telling her to go away. That's when we gave her the pill and put her in our bed. But," she said shaking her head, "I was so concerned with Lori that I ignored Cindy who had been saying all the while, 'It's my fault. I'm sorry.' I was too upset to talk to her and sent her back to bed." Aunt Pat was weeping now and Grandma and Uncle George tried to comfort her.

"I thought it best that we wait until morning to talk to Cindy," Grandma said.

"So did I," George agreed. "I thought the girls could explain more rationally in the morning. They weren't making much sense in the middle of the night."

"But we shouldn't have sent that little girl back down to that dark basement all by herself," Grandpa said as he rose to get the coffee pot.

"The baby woke up at about five," Aunt Pat continued. "I changed him, gave him a bottle and then started to think about Cindy all alone in the basement. I went down to see if she was all right, but she wasn't there!"

"We've looked all over—every place we could think of up and down the river and toward town," Mary Jo's father went on. "But we couldn't find her. We called Ken and Marie at Pine Ridge—they'll be here in a few hours. Then we called the sheriff."

"Mary Jo," Charlene said softly, "You're going to have to tell us why Lori was so upset and what made Cindy run away."

Mary Jo took a deep breath, nodded and spoke. "It all started because of the mysterious way your car horn honked, Uncle George. We talked about it the next day and decided that the reason it didn't happen here was because the Sioux and the white man's spirits together were stronger than the Hopi ones. Then we started talking about chichis, hoohoos and bogeymen. We decided that they were all kind of the same.

"We walked up to the old fort and decided to wade across the river because you," she motioned to all of the adults, "wouldn't have forbidden us to do that had we been boys. I knew Mark had done it when he was our age—you

expect boys to do things like that." She looked at Mark who looked down at the matchbook he was still fiddling with between nervous fingers.

"I guess we got mad at being treated so different. So we took off our shoes and socks and then our jeans because we knew if we got them wet, you'd know we'd been in the river.

"When we waded across, Lori almost fell in 'cause she's so short and the current was pulling at our legs. On the other side we walked up the path through the trees and saw an old shack. A strange man came out and started walking toward us. He was so scary that we ran. Lori got her braid caught in a tree, but we got her loose and all three of us got back across the river okay.

"We didn't dare tell about the man 'cause then you'd know we'd waded across the river when you told us not to," Mary Jo said to her grandmother. "We put our dry jeans on and I took our wet underpants home and washed and dried them." She looked uneasily at her mother who only nodded.

"Well, we called the man a chichi hoohoo bogeyman because he was so weird and scary.

"Then yesterday, when Grandpa let us take the canoe out by ourselves, we paddled up to the old fort again. It was hard work going upstream, just like you said it would be, Grandpa, so when we got to the fort and the shallow water, we decided to rest. Lori didn't want to, but Cindy and I were tired so we beached the canoe even though Grandpa told us not to.

"Cindy was thirsty and remembered seeing a pump at the house where the chi—strange man lived. She started to walk there and Lori and I didn't want her to go by herself, so we went along. The man came out. We ran and he followed us," she shivered as she remembered how frightened she had been. "He grabbed for Lori's braids but I pulled her away. Cindy threw a branch at him and he fell down. We got in the canoe and got away. Cindy talked us into not telling about the man because then Grandpa would know we had disobeyed him and wouldn't let us take the canoe out again."

Mary Jo hung her head and tears trickled down to her shirt, soaking the front. "We should have told—it wasn't all Cindy's fault. I knew how frightened Lori was."

"Then I came home and had to tell my story about the car horn honking," Uncle George said quietly.

Mary Jo nodded. "I even had a bad dream about that, falling in the river—all mixed up with that man."

"The man you saw, Mary Jo," Grandpa said, "is Andy Lytton. He's a deaf mute—he can't hear or speak and he is retarded. But he's harmless . . . I think." Grandpa stood and reached for his hat on the table. "We saw him this morning when we were looking for Cindy. He showed us the bruise on his leg and tried to tell us something but none of us could understand his finger talk. I'm going to get his sister Agnes to talk to him. Maybe he knows where Cindy is." He left the house.

"What is Andy doing all by himself in that old shack?" Mary Jo's mother asked. "I thought he lived in Sisseton with his brother."

"He sometimes comes here to visit Agnes," Grandma said, "but I don't think he's been here for the last year or two. I remember hearing that he had been ill. I can't imagine Agnes letting him stay by himself in the old river place.

That's where he and his brother and sister lived when they were children," she explained to Mary Jo. "I bet you girls frightened him as much as he did you." She went to the refrigerator.

"I'm going to make breakfast. We'll all need food to get us through this day."

"I'll help," Charlene said rising from the table, "and you can set the table, Mary Jo."

Suddenly, the phone rang.

Everyone turned to stare at where it hung on the wall by the door. Mary Jo's father picked up the receiver.

"Hello . . . This is Frank Swenson, Cindy's uncle, . . . Where? . . . Is she all right?"

Mary Jo clutched the forks she was holding.

"I'll be right up to get her." Frank hung up the phone and turned smiling to the others. "Cindy's okay. The highway patrol found her walking on the highway west of town. She was going home to Pine Ridge." He started for the door. "She's at the sheriff's office."

"Oh, thank God," Grandma cried. "I'm coming too. Poor little girl." She grabbed a sweater hanging over her chair and went with Frank.

Murmurs of relief came from the others and Mary Jo went on putting the forks on the table until Mark said, "Hey, dummy, I'm not going to eat with those forks if you're going to cry all over them," and they all laughed.

When Grandpa returned, he blew his nose hard after he heard Cindy was safe. He cleared his throat a few times and told about Andy Lytton.

"Agnes didn't even know that Andy was here. She just

got back yesterday from visiting her daughter in Minneapolis. We drove out to the old place and Andy told her—talking with his fingers—that his brother had put him on the bus in Sisseton to come for a visit. He has taken the bus by himself before to visit, but this time Agnes wasn't at the depot to meet him. She had left before she got her brother's letter telling of Andy's arrival.

"So Andy just walked to Agnes's, got the key she kept hidden in her garage and went into the house. He stayed there a couple of days and when she didn't return, he took some food and blankets and went to the old river place. Apparently Agnes let him stay there once in a while on his summer visits. There's cooking things, an old kerosene stove, lamp and bed—enough stuff for him to get by on. Agnes said that Andy has always wanted to live there by himself, but she would never let him for fear he would hurt himself or fall in the river.

"But old Andy is smarter than anyone thought. He's been living there by himself for almost a week and was getting along fine until the girls found him." Grandpa looked at Mary Jo who was rinsing off the forks at the sink.

"Andy was afraid that the girls would tell where he was and he'd have to leave the place he loved. He knew they couldn't understand him and were frightened of him, although he didn't mean to scare them. He wanted to stop them and write them a note explaining—that's why he followed and made a grab at Lori. He gave up after Cindy threw the branch at him. This morning he again tried to tell us, but we couldn't understand him either and didn't give him a chance to write it out. Poor old guy," Grandpa shook his head.

"I remember him," Mark said. "I've seen him up at the old fort place but I never thought he was so scary. Boy, you girls are stupid," he said disgustedly to Mary Jo. "What's going to happen to him now?"

"Agnes took him home with her to clean him up. Then she's going to clean up the old house, stock it with food and let Andy stay there for the rest of the summer anyway."

The door opened and Grandma entered smiling and holding Cindy's hand. Cindy looked sheepishly around the room and tears streaked down her dirty face as everyone hugged and kissed her. But when Mary Jo threw her arms around her, Cindy said, "I got to ride in a highway patrol car."

5

Apology

"Weren't you scared?" Lori asked.

The cousins were sitting under the willow by the river working at their looms. Cindy looked up and nodded. "Sure, I was. But not as much as when I was laying all by myself in that dark old basement after everyone went to bed. You kept yelling at me to keep away from you and then Grandma and Aunt Pat told me to go to bed—I didn't think anybody wanted me here."

"Oh, Cindy," Lori sighed.

"Then I kept seeing chichis and hoohoos and bogeymen all over in the dark and every once in a while the little window in the basement would give off a flash from the lightning outside. So when it started to get light I got up, dressed and decided to go home."

"Did you really think you could walk all the way to Pine Ridge by yourself?" Mary Jo asked.

"I don't know," Cindy shrugged. "But when the patrol car stopped me I was glad to get in. I was getting tired and it was damp even though the rain had stopped. I also knew that everybody would be wondering where I was. But," she said almost proudly, "I never thought that you'd think I was drowned and drag the river for me." Then she added, "Mom and Dad were sure mad when they got here, after driving like crazy all the way from Pine Ridge."

"But they were glad you were okay," Lori said.

"I guess so," Cindy shrugged. "But I have to go home with them today after our party instead of waiting to go with you, Lori, on Sunday."

"We're going home to the mesa tomorrow and we're not going to move to Aberdeen." Lori smiled happily at her cousins.

"Why not?" Mary Jo asked.

"Mom and Dad didn't give any reason except Dad decided not to take the job in Aberdeen. I'm glad," Lori said taking her finished potholder from her loom. "I would miss going to the mesa."

"I bet it's because of those spirits," Cindy said.

"Oh, let's don't start that again," said Mary Jo and the girls laughed.

"Hey, you three twerps," Mark called as he walked from the house. "It's time for your cake."

The cousins put their looms back in the box and Cindy carried it to the house. Today was their combined birthday party and they could officially call themselves eleven-year-olds. Still, Lori held back as they moved toward the crowd gathered around the picnic table.

"He still makes me feel creepy," she said staring at the old man who sat at one end of the table.

"Don't be silly. We know now that he wouldn't hurt us or anybody," Mary Jo said.

"I know, but it's going to be hard to shake his hand like Grandpa told us to."

"Don't worry," Cindy scowled. "If he grabs your braids I'll hit him with a loom."

The girls giggled, but all three made their way slowly and shyly toward Andy Lytton who was smiling and nodding at them. Grandpa had decided that Andy should be included in the birthday celebration to make amends for the girls' treatment of the old man. They were supposed to shake his hand and apologize.

Cindy put the box down and looked at her cousins who hung back. She wiped her hands on the skirt of her dress and walked up to Andy.

His smile widened and his eyes twinkled. "How could we ever have been scared of him?" Mary Jo wondered as she saw that his hair had been trimmed, his stubble beard shaved and that he was wearing a clean green shirt and brown trousers.

Cindy held out her hand and he took it. "Hello," she said. "I'm sorry I hit you with the tree branch."

He watched her lips, then nodded and let her hand go. Mary Jo was next. "Hello. I'm sorry we ran away from you."

Lori followed. Her voice quavered as she repeated Mary Jo's words and her hand trembled as she held it out.

Andy ceased smiling. Gently he reached out and touched one of Lori's long braids and then his fingers moved rapidly.

"He says," Andy's sister Agnes interpreted, "that he is sorry that he frightened you and he is glad that he is not a chichi hoohoo bogeyman."

University of Nebraska Press

ADVENTURES IN THE WEST
Stories for Young Readers
Edited by Susanne George Bloomfield and Eric Melvin Reed

Before MP3 players, DVDs, and video games, before even TV and radio, American children entertained themselves by reading. Often what they read were popular magazines aimed at the whole family; a weekly newspaper such as *The Youth's Companion* or a monthly magazine such as *St. Nicholas* were about all a turn-of-the-century family could afford. But what these publications provided was invaluable, and it is this education in imagination and American life that *Adventures in the West* revisits.

ISBN: 978-0-8032-5974-4 (paper)

LANA'S LAKOTA MOONS
By Virginia Driving Hawk Sneve

Lori is a quiet, contemplative bookworm. Lana is an outspoken adventuress. Different as they are, they are first cousins, sisters in the Lakota way. And when both befriend a Hmong girl new to their school, the discovery of a culture so strange to them and so rich with possibilities brings them together as never before in an experience of life and loss. As the girls learn of the moons of the Lakota calendar, they also learn that the circle of life is never broken, even when death comes to one of them.

ISBN: 978-0-8032-6028-3 (paper)

BEAVER STEALS FIRE
A Salish Coyote Story
By the Confederated Salish and Kootenai Tribes
Illustrated by Sam Sandoval

Beaver Steals Fire is an ancient and powerful tale springing from the hearts and experiences of the Salish people of Montana. Steeped in the rich and culturally vital storytelling tradition of the tribe, this tale teaches both respect for fire and awareness of its significance, themes particularly relevant today. This unforgettable version of the story is told by Salish elder Johnny Arlee and beautifully illustrated by tribal artist Sam Sandoval.

ISBN: 978-0-8032-1640-2 (paper)

Order online at www.nebraskapress.unl.edu or call 1-800-755-1105.
Mention the code "BOFOX" to receive a 20% discount.